MW00764953

A House for Patches

By Eduardo Díaz
Illustrated by Pat Paris

Copyright © 2000 Metropolitan Teaching and Learning Company.
Published by Metropolitan Teaching and Learning Company.
Printed in the United States of America.
All rights reserved. No part of this publication may be reproduced or utilized in any form or by any means, electronic or mechanical, including photocopying, recording, or by any information storage and retrieval system without permission in writing from the publisher. For information regarding permission, write to Metropolitan Teaching and Learning Company, 33 Irving Place, New York, NY 10003.
ISBN 1-58120-053-6

1 2 3 4 5 6 7 8 9 CL 03 02 01 00

"I have big news!" said Jed. "Lin's mom bought her a new dog. She's going to pick him up after school."

"That is cool," said Dan. "Lin has waited a long time for a dog."

"I wish we could get a dog," said Nina. "Tell us about Lin's new dog. What is it like? Is it a big dog?"

"I have just a few clues," said Jed. "Lin said that his fur is white with patches of black. There's a big black patch on his back. His fur is smooth and he has a long tail. Lin named him Patches. I don't know if he's big or small. But Lin said he's a very nice dog."

"When can we see Patches?" asked Nina.

"We have to wait, but we'll see him soon," said Jed. "First, Lin wants some time to get to know Patches. He needs to go to the vet, too. Lin is going to give him a big party soon. We can all go. I got Patches a present. It's a big blue brush. Dogs like to have their fur brushed."

"A party for a dog. Cool!" said Nina. "What can we give Patches? We need to get him a present, Dan. It has to be a great present."

"We have an old doghouse in the workroom. We can fix it up for Patches," said Dan.

"How do we do that?" asked Nina.

"I don't have a clue," said Dan. "But we can ask Dad. He'll help us."

"This is the workroom," said Dan. "All the stuff we need is right here. There are tools, glue, sandpaper, and screws."

"This is a cool room," said Jed. "It will be fun to fix up that doghouse."

"Here is the old doghouse," said Dad. "It has a scratch or two and a few bumps. The wood doesn't look even. We have to glue some of it back. It will take some work to make it look like new. You can all help. I'll get the tools."

"The doghouse is a mess," said Nina. "It will not make a very good present."

"If we fix it up, it will look good," said Dan. "Dad, this doghouse has scratches all over it. How can we smooth them out?"

"I'll show you," said Dad. "We'll sand it down first. I'll get some sandpaper. I'll rub the sandpaper over the side to make it smooth."

"Can I have some sandpaper, too?" asked Nina.

"Sure," said Dad. "Now take your sandpaper and rub the side of the doghouse. As you rub, the scratches and the old paint will come off. Dan and Jed, you two can sand the sides of the doghouse, too. Soon this doghouse will look like new. You'll see."

"My side looks very smooth," said Nina.

"No more scratches on this side. The wood is smooth. Even the old paint came off," said Jed. "This doghouse looks a lot better."

"Can I use a tool now?" asked Nina.

"Wait," said Dad. "First we have more work to do. We need to glue this wood back and put some new screws in. Get the glue, Dan. Put a little bit here. Jed, check the other side. Is there wood on that side that needs glue?"

"This side needs glue, too," said Jed. "Just here and there."

"Here is the glue," said Dan. "Make sure it doesn't drip. It will make a mess."

"The doghouse looks better," said Nina, "But it still looks old. What can we do to make it look new, Dad?"

"We still have to paint the doghouse. That is a job you can help with," said Dad.

"I'll look for more paint," said Dad. "It's in the other room. Dan, you look for the other brushes. Jed, you put down more paper. We don't want to drip paint in the workroom."

"What color paint do we have?" asked Nina.

"We have blue, red, and white paint," said Dad. "Should I mix the blue paint? Would Patches like a blue doghouse?"

"Blue is a great color," said Nina. "Mix it up. Patches will like a blue doghouse."

"We can use some red paint on top," said Dan. "Look out with your brushes. We don't want paint to drip all over."

"You're doing a very good job, Nina," said Jed. "Your side looks very good."

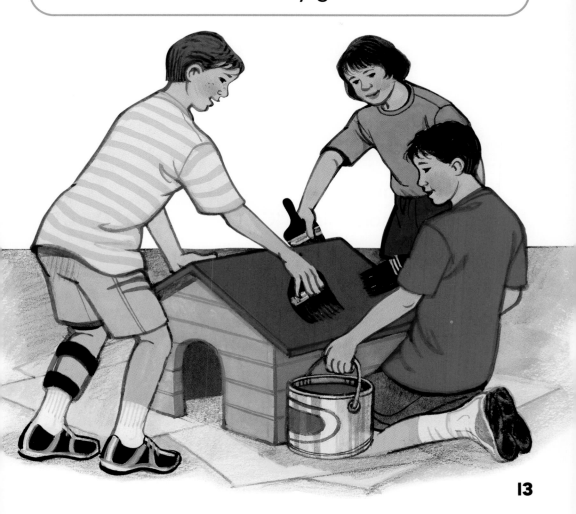

"Patches should have his name on the doghouse," said Nina. "Can we do that, Dad?"

"Sure we can," said Dad. "We mixed the red paint. Here is some wood. You can paint his name on it. After you paint, we'll screw the wood to the doghouse. I'll go look for a few screws."

"This will be the best present yet," said Nina. "Patches will even have his name on it."

"This is one cool doghouse," said Jed. "That is for sure. We did a great job of fixing it up."

"There's just one thing," said Dan. "The doghouse has one small room. How big is Patches, Jed? What if he doesn't fit?"

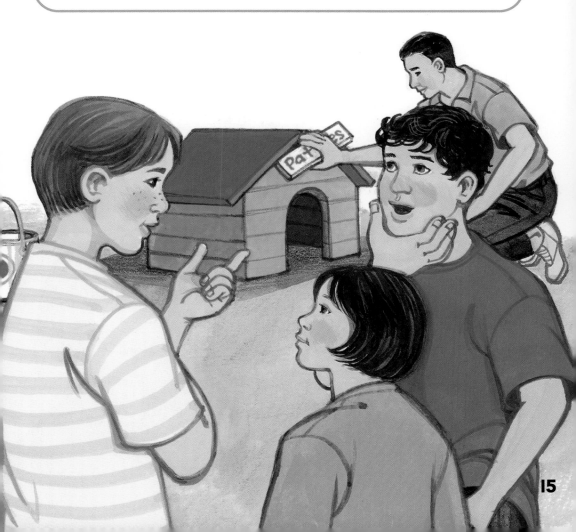

"Don't ask me," said Jed. "I don't have a clue. We'll have to wait and see. I just know he has a long tail."

"What if his tail can't fit inside?" asked Dan.

"Then we'll be in the doghouse," said Nina.